Michael Bond

The Giant Paddington Story Book

GALLERY BOOKS
An Imprint of W. H. Smith Publishers Inc.
112 Madison Avenue
New York City 10016

The stories in this book are based on the television films. They have been specially written by Michael Bond for younger children.

Paddington Does It Himself and Paddington in the Kitchen come from PADDINGTON HELPS OUT

Paddington's Birthday Party comes from A BEAR CALLED PADDINGTON

Paddington Hits Out comes from PADDINGTON GOES TO TOWN

Paddington On The River comes from COMINGS AND GOINGS AT NUMBER 32

The stories in this book originally published by Carnival 1989

This edition published in 1989 by Gallery Books, an imprint of W.H. Smith Publishers, Inc., 112 Madison Avenue, New York 10016

Gallery Books are available for bulk purchase for sales promotions and premium use. For details write or telephone the Manager of Special Sales, W.H. Smith Publishers, Inc., 112 Madison Avenue, New York, 10016. (212) 532-6600

ISBN 0 8317 3968 1

Printed and bound in Great Britain by Collins, Glasgow.

Paddington

CONTENTS

Paddington
Does It Himself

One day, the Browns had to go out early in order to do some shopping, so Paddington decided to have his breakfast in bed.

Paddington liked having breakfast in bed. It gave him a chance to catch up on his reading, and as a special treat Mrs. Brown left him a pile of books and magazines.

Some of them were very interesting indeed and one in particular made him sit up and take notice.

It was called "DO-IT-YOURSELF" and it showed how to make a magazine rack.

Although the article didn't say anything about "bears" doing it themselves, it made it all sound very simple.

In fact, it was so interesting, Paddington dipped his paw in the hot cocoa by mistake instead of the marmalade jar.

All of which helped him make up his mind. He would have a go himself.

Paddington wasn't the sort of bear who believed in wasting time, and he decided it wasn't worth having a proper wash if he was going to get dirty again. So, apart from cleaning his teeth, he simply passed the face flannel over his whiskers a couple of times.

Only a few days before, he'd accidentally bought a set of carpentry tools at an auction sale, and since then they had been standing idle in Mr. Brown's shed. Now seemed a very good time to test them out.

Paddington investigated the contents of the tool box. There was a hammer, a saw, three chisels, a plane and several other things which he didn't recognise. Altogether it seemed very good value and he felt sure he would be able to make the Browns a very nice magazine rack indeed.

A few moments later, armed with a piece of plywood Mr. Brown had promised he could use, Paddington staggered outside.

Almost at once he wished he hadn't, for there was a strong wind blowing and he was so laden it wasn't at all easy which was how he came to bump into the Brown's neighbour, Mr. Curry.

"Bear!" bellowed Mr. Curry. "What are you doing, bear?"

"Do it yourself, Mr. Curry!" exclaimed Paddington.

"Don't be impertinent, bear!" roared Mr. Curry.

"Oh, no, Mr. Curry," replied Paddington hastily. "I didn't mean you were to do it *your*self. I meant I'm going to do it *my*self. I'm making a magazine rack. Look. . . ."

. . . And he held up the book for Mr. Curry to see.

"Mm." Mr. Curry calmed down slightly. "A magazine rack, eh?" he said thoughtfully. "I'd like one of those, bear."

"As it happens," he went on, "I'm going out, so you can use my kitchen table to work on. If you make me one by the time I get back I *may* not report you for banging my nose just now."

"Thank you very much, Mr. Curry," said Paddington gloomily.

He wasn't too keen on doing jobs for the Browns' neighbour. Somehow or other they always seemed to go wrong.

Before he went out, Mr. Curry gave Paddington a long list of "don'ts" – mostly to do with not making a mess, but as Paddington set to work he quickly forgot them in his excitement.

Paddington had never sawn anything in two before and he found it wasn't as easy as it looked.

In fact, it got harder and harder.

He tried starting from the other side, but that was just as bad.

It wasn't until he stopped for a much needed rest that he discovered why.

There was a splintering noise and the table suddenly parted in the middle.

Paddington tried hard to think of a reason why Mr. Curry might like two small tables with only two legs each instead of one large table with four legs.

He peered hopefully at his instructions, but there was nothing in them about mending next-door neighbours' tables which had been accidentally sawn in half.

Paddington wasn't the sort of bear to be beaten, so after carefully spreading some glue along the edge of the two halves he tried propping them up on some cardboard boxes, nailing them both together for good measure.

To finish things off, he rubbed some marmalade along the join in the hope that it would disguise the crack.

But even with the curtains drawn he had to admit that Mr. Curry's table still had a nasty sag in the middle.

Worse still, it was *very* wobbly.
Paddington decided he had an emergency on his paws.

First he sawed a piece of wood off the longest leg, but that made the table wobble in the other direction.

So he tried sawing the end off one of the other legs, but that only made matters worse.

Paddington lost count of the number of pieces he sawed off the legs, and it wasn't until he stood up again that he had yet another shock.

Mr. Curry's table seemed to have shrunk. In fact, he couldn't remember ever having seen such a short table before.

He looked in the book and saw an article headed, "Delight Your Family and Surprise Your Friends".

Paddington was quite sure Mr. Curry would be surprised when he saw what was left of his table, but as for delighting the Browns with a magazine rack . . . that seemed very far away.

It was much, much later that morning when he finally got back to the Browns' house, but when she saw what he'd made them, Mrs. Bird was more than delighted.

"Most useful," she said. "Now perhaps the room won't get so untidy."

"And how kind of you to make two," added Mrs. Brown.

"Er . . . well . . ." said Paddington. "I'm afraid they're not *both* for you. One's really for Mr. Curry, but I think I'll leave it on his doorstep after dark."

"After dark?" repeated Judy. "Whatever for?"

"I think I can guess," said Jonathan. "Look!"

Everybody hurried to the window in order to see what was going on outside.

"Bear!" roared Mr. Curry. "Where are you, bear?"

"Well, Paddington," said Mrs. Bird. "What have you got to say?"

"Perhaps," said Paddington hopefully, "Mr. Curry will feel better if I make him a present of my tools as well as the magazine rack.

"After to-day I don't think I shall be 'doing it myself' again for a long time!"

Paddington
in the Kitchen

One morning, Mr. and Mrs. Brown woke feeling ill . . . so they went straight back to bed.

"The trouble is," said Mrs. Brown, "with Jonathan and Judy at school and Mrs. Bird on holiday, who's going to look after us?"

"Don't worry, Mrs. Brown," exclaimed Paddington. "I'll do it! Bears are good at looking after people."

"I'll make you a stew," he announced, as he left the room. "Aunt Lucy always made me a stew when I wasn't well."

"Oh, dear!" groaned Mr. Brown. "I think I suddenly feel worse again!"

Paddington hurried downstairs as fast as his legs would carry him. He was very keen on cooking; at least, he always felt he would be if he ever got the chance.

He'd often watched Mrs. Bird at work in her kitchen and although he'd never actually made a stew himself before, she always made it look very easy. He couldn't wait to have a go.

First of all, he cut up some meat and put it into a saucepan.

Then he added a pawful of carrots, some water and several onions for good measure.

After he'd put the saucepan on the stove to boil, Paddington turned his attention to the important matter of the dumplings.

Mrs. Bird made very good stews. If he had any complaints at all it was that her dumplings were a little on the small side.

Paddington decided that *his* dumplings would be the biggest ever made.

It was some while before the cloud of flour finally settled, but when it had, he added a generous helping of suet followed by a jug of milk.

It was when he came to stir the mixture that Paddington first began to feel worried. The spoon went into the bowl easily enough but once in, it didn't seem to want to move.

In fact, far from being able to *stir* the mixture, Paddington began to wonder if he would ever get the spoon out again.

He didn't remember Mrs. Bird having so much trouble with *her* dumplings and he began to wish he'd consulted one of her recipe books first.

Paddington decided to make the best of a bad job. He took the saucepan of stew off the stove and tried to empty his dumpling mixture into it.

But the bowl was a lot heavier than he'd expected and no matter how hard he shook it, nothing seemed to happen.

He decided the only thing to do was to give the basin a sharp tap with Mrs. Bird's rolling pin.

But he soon wished he hadn't.

For a moment, Paddington toyed with the idea of hollowing out the dumpling mixture and making it in a new basin to replace the one he'd broken, but matters were suddenly decided for him as the lump of dough slid into the stew with a loud "plop".

But Paddington's troubles weren't over by a long way. Far from it being *in* the saucepan, half the dumpling mixture was sticking out of the top. And for some strange reason it seemed to be growing larger with every passing moment.

In fact, it had grown so much even his hat wasn't big enough to take it all.

In the end, Paddington decided to do what Mr. Brown always did with the family suitcase when they went on holiday he stood on the lid!

The saucepan was now so heavy Paddington wasn't at all sure how he managed to get it back on to the stove, but he was so worn out he didn't really care.

After mopping his brow with a tea towel, he sat down in the middle of the kitchen floor and closed his eyes. A few seconds later some loud snores added themselves to the sound of bubbling stew.

Paddington wasn't sure how long he slept, but he woke with a nasty feeling that he wasn't alone. SOMETHING was in the room with him and it was getting nearer . . . and nearer.

Just as he began to think that perhaps he was in the middle of a nightmare, there was a loud crash from the direction of the stove and something rolled across the floor towards him.

Paddington was a brave bear at heart, but he didn't stay to see what it was. Instead, he beat a hasty retreat in the direction of the garden.

He felt it would be better to investigate the matter from the other side of the window.

It wasn't until much later that morning that Mr. Brown happened to look out of the bedroom window. As he did so he gave a start.

"That's funny," he exclaimed. "There's a big white thing in the garden. Come and have a look. I'm sure it wasn't there just now."

Mrs. Brown joined her husband at the window. Sure enough, standing in the middle of the rockery, was a large, white object.

"Whatever can it be, Henry?" she asked.

"Do *you* know what it is, Paddington?" asked Mr. Brown, as the door opened and a small figure in a duffle coat came into the room carrying a tray laden with food.

"Perhaps it's a snowball, Mr. Brown," said Paddington innocently.

"In midsummer!" exclaimed Mrs. Brown.

"Well, whatever it is," said Mr. Brown, "those birds don't seem to think much of it. I think one of them has just broken its beak."

"In that case," said Paddington hastily, as he placed the tray between the two beds, "I think you should hurry up and eat yours before it sets!"

Mr. and Mrs. Brown exchanged glances, "Before it *sets*!" repeated Mr. Brown. "I don't like the sound of that!"

"Neither do I," agreed Mrs. Brown nervously.

"Well," said Paddington, playing for time while the others got back into bed. "I'm afraid I've been having trouble with my dumplings, but don't worry . . . I've got some spare mixture. It's under my . . . Oh! Oh, dear!"

"*Now* what's the matter?" asked Mr. Brown. For some strange reason, Paddington seemed to be having trouble taking his hat off.

"Well," gasped Paddington, "you may want some 'seconds', Mr. Brown, and I wouldn't want to disappoint you.

"There's nothing worse than being without dumplings. Especially when you're ill!"

Paddington's
Birthday Party

No one, not even Paddington, knew quite how old he was when he arrived at number thirty-two Windsor Gardens, so the Browns decided to start again and call him "one".

Everyone agreed with Mrs. Bird when she said they ought to celebrate the occasion by holding a birthday party.

Paddington had lots of presents, but his favourite one of all was a conjuring outfit from Mr. and Mrs. Brown. It came from Barkridges and it not only had a table and a large box for making things disappear, but there was a special magic wand and a book of instructions as well.

Unfortunately, before he had time to try out any of the tricks, the guests began to arrive and he hurried downstairs to greet them.

His friend, Mr. Gruber, who kept an antique shop in the market, was the first to arrive, and he was closely followed by the Browns' bad-tempered neighbour, Mr. Curry.

Mr. Gruber was always welcome, but Mr. Curry hadn't even been invited.

"I bet he's only after the free tea," hissed Jonathan.

Luckily, Mrs. Bird's teas were usually so ample there was more than enough for everyone — including uninvited guests. So even Mr. Curry had no cause to complain.

In fact, everyone voted it the best tea they'd ever had, and Paddington himself was so full he had a job finding enough breath to blow out the candle. But at last he managed it without singeing his whiskers, and everyone clapped and wished him a Happy Birthday.

After tea, Paddington announced that he had a special surprise for everyone. Then he disappeared upstairs to his room in order to get ready for it.

While Mrs. Brown and Mrs. Bird cleared away the tea things, Mr. Brown set about arranging the rest of the guests at the other end of the room.

No sooner had everyone settled down than the door opened and Paddington reappeared, staggering under the weight of his magic outfit.

"Ladies and gentlemen," he announced, when all was ready. "My next trick is impossible."

"But you haven't done *one* yet!" called Mr. Curry.

Paddington ignored the interruption. He consulted his instruction book.

"For this trick," he continued, "I would like an egg, please."

Mrs. Bird looked worried. "Oh, dear," she said. "Can't you use something else?"

"No," said Paddington firmly. "It definitely says an egg. I'm going to turn it into a bunch of flowers," he added darkly, ". . . if I can get my magic wand to work."

Paddington held up the magic wand and began making some passes over it with his other paw. To everyone's astonishment, including his own, it suddenly went quite limp.

"Quite good for a bear," said Mr. Curry over the applause. "Of course we all know it's joined by elastic in the middle . . . but quite good."

Paddington gave the Browns' neighbour a hard stare, but luckily Mrs. Bird came into the room at that moment carrying an egg.

"Do be careful," she warned. "I had the carpet cleaned only last week."

Paddington thanked Mrs. Bird, and then placed the egg on his magic table and covered it with a handkerchief. "Now," he announced, "if you watch closely you will see it turn into a bunch of flowers."

"I'd sooner you turned it into an omelette," called Mr. Curry. "I'm getting hungry again."

But Mr. Curry's words fell on deaf ears, for Paddington was much too busy getting ready for his trick.

He appeared to be doing something behind the table.

"I shall now say the magic word," he announced, tapping the mound under the handkerchief with his wand. "ABRA-CA-DABRA!"

As Paddington tapped at the handkerchief a murmur of approval went round the audience, for sure enough, the egg had disappeared.

"Bravo!" shouted Mr. Gruber.

"Good old Paddington!" cried Judy.

But Paddington was far from finished. Before the applause for the first half of his trick had died away he raised his hat and withdrew a bunch of roses.

Mr. Brown took a closer look at the crumpled objects in Paddington's paw. "Aren't those my roses?" he exclaimed.

"No wonder the bushes looked rather bare just now!"

"Shh, Henry," said Mrs. Brown. "I'm sure they'll straighten out again once they're in water.

"Besides, I think he's about to do another trick."

"Perhaps he's going to make himself disappear now," said Judy.

Everyone waited patiently for something to happen, but as the minutes ticked by they looked more and more uneasy.

"Do you think young Mr. Brown's all right in there?" asked Mr. Gruber at last.

"No, I'm not," cried Paddington. "It's all dark and I can't read my instructions."

Mr. Gruber hurried to Paddington's assistance.

"If I were you," he said, as Paddington crawled out, "I would try something simpler next time."

"Hear! Hear!" called Mr. Curry. "I didn't think much of that trick. I'd like to see something else."

Paddington thanked his friend and then peered at the instruction book again.

"There's a very good one here to do with a watch," he announced at last.

At the mention of the word "watch", everyone hastily pulled their cuffs down over their wrists. All, that is, except Mr. Curry, who had just spied a plate of sandwiches which had been overlooked.

"You wanted to see another trick," said Mrs. Bird pointedly. "Now's your chance!"

"Very well," said Mr. Curry with ill grace. "But make sure you look after it, bear. It's very valuable."

Paddington placed Mr. Curry's watch on the table, covered it carefully with the handkerchief, and then picked up a large mallet.

"This is a very good trick," he announced, as he hit the handkerchief several times as hard as he could. "It says so in the book."

"Now," continued Paddington. "I will lift up the corner of the handkerchief . . . so, and . . . oh! Oh, dear!"

"Oh, dear!" bellowed Mr. Curry. "What do you mean . . . *oh, dear?* What's happened, bear?"

Out of the corner of his eye Paddington caught sight of some ominous words in his book of instructions. "For this trick," it said, "it is necessary to use a *dummy* watch."

"I think perhaps I forgot to say ABRA-CADABRA, Mr. Curry," he faltered.

"ABRACADABRA!" thundered Mr. Curry as he stared at the remains of his watch. "ABRACADABRA! I'll give you ABRACA-DABRA! That was a very valuable antique. It was shockproof, *and* it had twenty jewels."

"It doesn't look very shockproof to me," said Mr. Brown.

"And it certainly isn't valuable," said Mr. Gruber. "Old it may be, but it's not an antique. I remember selling it to you years ago and you didn't pay me much for it then."

"I think I may have found one of the jewels, Mr. Curry," said Paddington excitedly.

"*One* of the jewels!" exlaimed Mr. Curry. "What about the other nineteen? This is disgraceful!"

Mr. Curry was so cross he flung himself down in his chair, and just as quickly he leapt up again. "Ugh!" he said. "I'm sitting on something sticky!"

"Oh, dear," said Paddington. "I think you've sat on my disappearing egg, Mr. Curry. It must have reappeared again!"

"Serves you right for telling lies to a young bear," said Mrs. Bird sternly. "Trying to make him think it was a valuable watch indeed!"

"Pah!" snorted Mr. Curry.

But for once the Browns' neighbour was at a loss for words. "I shall never," he said, glaring at Paddington as he made for the door, "ever come to one of your parties again!"

When the laughter had died down, Mr. Brown looked at his own watch. "It's getting very near bedtime," he said. "Most of all Paddington's, so I suggest we *all* do a disappearing trick now!"

"All good things come to an end," said Judy, as she and Jonathan joined Paddington on the doorstep of number thirty-two Windsor Gardens while he waved goodbye to everyone. "Even birthday parties."

"If they didn't," said Jonathan, "you'd never have another one to look forward to."

"Perhaps," said Paddington, as he went upstairs to bed, "I'd better write this one up in my scrapbook first before I forget it.

"Besides, I want to tell my Aunt Lucy all about it, and so much has happened I may have a job getting it all on one postcard!"

Paddington
Hits Out

One day Mr. Curry decided to enter a golf competition, and he asked Paddington to be his caddy.

"All you have to do, bear, is look after my clubs," he boomed.

Paddington wasn't very keen on doing things for the Browns' neighbour. They always seemed to go wrong. All the same, he felt most important as he took Mr. Curry's bag.

"I do hope he'll be all right," said Mrs. Brown anxiously, as Paddington set off next day. "You know how bad-tempered Mr. Curry gets, and golf isn't the easiest of games."

Mrs. Bird gave a snort. As far as she was concerned Mr. Curry deserved all he got. "He's for ever trying to get something for nothing," she said.

All the same, she began to look slightly worried as she waved goodbye. With Paddington let loose on a golf course there was no knowing what might happen.

By the time Paddington reached the golf club quite a large crowd had already collected, and several of them applauded as he made his way towards the first hole.

Paddington decided he liked golf courses and he raised his hat politely in return.

Even Arnold Parker, the world-famous golf champion, who was acting as judge, gave him a friendly salute.

"Good afternoon, Mr. Parker," called Paddington, returning the wave as he hurried on his way.

Mr. Curry was already waiting impatiently for him.

"Ah, there you are, bear," he growled. "I thought you were never coming."

"Now this is a very important part of the competition," he continued. "It's to see who can hit their ball the farthest. There's a special prize for the winner so I want you to make sure my ball doesn't get lost."

"Don't worry, Mr. Curry," said Paddington. "I've marked it with a special marmalade chunk. Look . . ."

"Are you sure it won't come off, bear?" growled Mr. Curry.

"*Quite* sure," said Paddington firmly, as he took up the position he'd seen Arnold Parker use. "Mrs. Bird says my chunks stick to anything ."

"Hm. Well, I hope you're right, bear," growled Mr. Curry. "If you're not . . ." He broke off as a loud cracking noise came from Paddington's direction.

"Bear!" he bellowed. "That's my best club you've broken! How dare you! Wait until we get back. You won't hear the last of this!"

"Perhaps you could tie the two ends together, Mr. Curry?" said Paddington hopefully.

"Tie the two ends together!" spluttered Mr. Curry. "Why . . . I've . . ." He broke off as he caught sight of someone coming their way.

"Well?" he demanded. "What do *you* want?"

Paddington jumped to his feet. "Hello, Mr. Parker," he exclaimed. "I'm afraid I've been having trouble with one of Mr. Curry's clubs!"

"Oh, dear," said Arnold Parker. "You're welcome to borrow mine if you like."

"Parker," exclaimed Mr. Curry. "Not *the* Arnold Parker? I had no idea you two knew each other. You didn't tell me, bear."

"Of course, I was only joking just now," he continued, rubbing his hands in invisible soap.

"Remind me to give you five pence when we get home!"

"Any friend of yours, bear, is a friend of mine," said Mr. Curry.

"Now, have you got my tee?"

"Your tea, Mr. Curry?"

Anxious to make amends while the Browns' neighbour was in a good mood, Paddington peered in the bag, but it seemed to be empty.

"You can have a marmalade sandwich if you like," he announced, removing a shapeless white object from inside his hat. "I brought it in case I had an emergency."

"Bah!" snorted Mr. Curry, his bad temper getting the better of him again. "I don't mean the sort of tea you eat . . . I want it to put my ball on so that I can address it."

Paddington began to look more and more confused. He'd never heard of anyone hitting a ball off a marmalade sandwich before, let alone writing their address on it.

Arnold Parker gave a cough. "I think," he said, handing Mr. Curry a small yellow object, "your friend wants one of these. It's what we golfers call a tee. It's to stand your ball on. When we get ready to hit it we say we're addressing it."

It seemed to Paddington a very complicated way to go about hitting a small ball with a piece of metal on the end of a stick.

All the same, as Mr. Curry lifted his club and Arnold Parker hissed a word of warning, he did as he was told and hurried off to take cover behind a nearby sand dune.

But he'd barely gone a couple of steps when he was stopped dead in his tracks by a loud cry from Mr. Curry. And when he looked round he saw why.

Mr. Curry appeared to be turning a cartwheel.

"Oh, dear," said Arnold Parker. "I think you've trodden on your friend's marmalade sandwich."

"Bah!" bellowed Mr. Curry. "I've hurt my leg. Now I shan't be able to play. It's all your fault, bear!"

"Perhaps," said Paddington, "I could do it for you, Mr. Curry. Bears are good at hitting things. Besides, your club is just the right length now."

"A good idea," said Arnold Parker. "There's nothing in the rules to say bears can't take part in the competition. Why not?"

Mr. Curry gazed at Paddington, then at the ball, still lying where he'd placed it.

He looked as if he could have thought of a good many reasons why not, but the rattle of an approaching goods train made him change his mind.

"All right, bear," he growled. "But watch what you're doing."

Paddington needed no second bidding. Before Mr. Curry had time to change his mind, he'd taken careful aim and with a satisfying clunk the ball went sailing into the air.

"Fore!" shouted Arnold Parker, above the roar of the train.

"Five!" cried Paddington excitedly.

He'd never hit a golf ball before and although it hadn't quite gone in the direction he'd intended, he could hardly believe his good fortune at doing so well.

"Congratulations!" said Arnold Parker as he picked himself up. "Did anyone see where it went?"

"I did," bellowed Mr. Curry. "It went over there . . . towards the railway line. And if it's been run over by that train . . . I'll . . . I'll . . ."

Paddington never did learn what Mr. Curry would have done had his golf ball been run over, for as luck would have it something very strange happened. Something even Mr. Curry couldn't grumble at especially when he found himself being presented with a brand new set of golf clubs later that day.

"Do you mean to say I've won these?" he exclaimed.

"No," said Mrs. Bird. "*Paddington* did, but he's giving them to you to make up for breaking yours."

"Your ball went nine miles," said Judy proudly.

"Arnold Parker says it must be a world record," added Jonathan. "I bet the engine driver was surprised."

"*Nine* miles?" repeated Mr. Curry. "*Engine* driver? What *are* you talking about?"

"Your ball landed in that goods train by mistake, Mr. Curry," explained Paddington. "The driver sent it back from the next station, and Mr. Parker said there was nothing in the rules to stop it being counted. So I won first prize."

"Bears," said Mrs. Bird, "always fall on their feet."

"That's what Mr. Parker said," agreed Paddington. "He's going to put marmalade chunks on *all* his golf balls in future . . . just like this one. He thinks it might bring him luck.

"I should do the same to yours, Mr. Curry. Besides, if you ever get lost in a bunker at least you won't go hungry."

Paddington
On the River

One morning, Paddington was woken early by the sound of voices. They seemed to be coming from somewhere outside his window, and as he climbed out of bed he helped himself to some marmalade — just to make sure he wasn't still dreaming.

When he peered out of his window he found to his surprise that all the Brown family were gathered round a large box-like object in the middle of the lawn.

It was all very mysterious and it definitely needed investigating; so without further ado, he put on his duffle-coat and hurried downstairs.

He joined the others just as Mrs. Bird was shutting the lid on a large wicker basket.

"Trust Paddington!" said Jonathan.

"It was meant to be a surprise," groaned Judy.

"Don't worry, Paddington!" laughed Mrs. Brown, when she saw the look on his face. "We're only going for a picnic on the river."

"And guess what?" said Judy. "Daddy's giving a prize to whoever catches the first fish of the day!"

Paddington had never been on a picnic before, let alone on a river, and he was very excited.

He had a quick bath and then, while Jonathan and Judy looked for some fishing nets, he made a special sandwich with the rest of his marmalade and put it under his hat in case of an emergency.

It was a very gay party of Browns who arrived at the boathouse.

"I'll put you in charge of the pole, Paddington," called Mr. Brown, as they climbed into a punt.

"Thank you very much, Mr. Brown," said Paddington. "Bears are good at poles."

"Right!" called Mr. Brown, when they were all settled. "Cast off! Anchors aweigh!"

"Do *what*, Mr. Brown?" called Paddington.

"Put the end of the pole in the water and push," shouted Jonathan.

"Oh, dear," said Mrs. Brown, as the boat began to move. "I'm sure something awful is going to happen. . . ."

Paddington did as he was told, and as soon as he felt the end of the pole touch bottom he shoved at it with all his might.

The words were hardly out of her mouth when her worst fears were realised.

Paddington discovered it was one thing pushing a pole into the bed of a river, but quite another matter getting it out again.

It was well and truly stuck in the mud.

"**H**elp!" he cried, as he felt the punt glide away from under him.

"Mercy me!" cried Mrs. Bird.

"*Do* something, Henry!" gasped Mrs. Brown.

"*Do* something?" said Mr. Brown crossly. "What *can* I do? Paddington's got the pole!"

"Hold on, Paddington!" shouted Jonathan.

"Hold on to *what*?" gasped Paddington, as he came up for air.

Mrs. Bird lowered her sunshade.

"We'd best be using this as a paddle," she said. "I'm not sure if that bear can swim!"

At the sound of her words, Paddington gave another cry of alarm.

"I don't think I can, Mrs. Bird," he cried, and promptly sank again.

Luckily he was near the bank and some passers-by rushed to his rescue.

Soon Paddington had quite a crowd round him.

"The thing is," said a man, "'oo's going to be the first to give 'im the kiss of life?"

"Perhaps," said another man, when no one answered, "we should try artificial respiration?"

Paddington sat up.

"*Artificial* respiration!" he exclaimed hotly. "I'd rather have the real thing if you don't mind."

While he was talking, Paddington reached up to adjust his hat; and as he did so he had yet another shock.

There was nothing on his head to adjust!"

"Oh, dear," said a man, as Paddington fell over backwards in alarm. "He's lost his balance. Perhaps it's delayed shock."

"I haven't lost my balance!" said Paddington, giving the man a hard stare. "I've lost my hat. It's a very valuable one. There isn't another one like it in the world."

"Perhaps it's sunk?" suggested someone in the crowd.

"Or got swep' over the weir," said another, gloomily.

Paddington scrambled to his feet.

"My hat . . . swep' over a weir!" he exclaimed, hardly able to believe his ears.

"Don't worry, Paddington!" called Judy, as the Browns' boat drifted closer to the bank. "We'll find it."

"Jump on board," shouted Jonathan. "We'll give you a lift to the lock."

"I think," he announced over his shoulder, "I'd sooner stick to dry land, if you don't mind. It's much quicker and it's a lot safer."

Paddington considered the matter for a moment before setting off in great haste down the towpath.

"I knew Paddington would be upset," said Mrs. Bird, as the Browns made haste to follow him.

"He had a special bath this morning and *two* in one day is more than enough for any bear — even if one of them was an accident."

"A *hat*?" repeated the lock-keeper, when Paddington reported his loss.

"What sort of a hat?"

"It's a family heirloom," said Paddington, "and it's very special. It was handed down to me by my uncle and I've worn it ever since I left Darkest Peru."

The lock-keeper looked most impressed. "I don't think I've ever had anything from Darkest Peru over my weir before," he said.

"It wouldn't be that thing in the bucket, would it? We fished it out just now." He gave a shudder. "All dark and shapeless, it was."

"That *sounds* like it," said Mrs. Brown, as she arrived on the scene.

"I do hope so," said Mrs. Bird. "We shall never hear the last of it if it isn't."

Paddington lifted the object out of the bucket and held it up.

"It *is* my hat," he announced, much to everyone's relief.

"You can tell it's mine," he added, as he removed the remains of something white, "because it's got a marmalade sandwich inside. At least, what's left of it!"

He glanced down into the bucket again and as he did so, he nearly fell over backwards with surprise.

"Guess what, Mr. Brown!" he exclaimed excitedly. "I think I may have won the prize for the first catch of the day."

"Good heavens!" Mr. Brown joined Paddington at the bucket. "He's right, you know. Come and have a look, everyone."

Sure enough, as the others gathered round the bucket they could see, not one, but two fish swimming in and out of the weed at the bottom.

"You just can't compete with *that*," said Jonathan.

"*And* he got a free hat-wash into the bargain," agreed Judy.

"I expect that's how he caught the fish in the first place," remarked Mrs. Brown. "They probably swam into it by mistake."

"I expect they were hungry," said Mrs. Bird. "Fish like nibbling a piece of bread."

Paddington suddenly had second thoughts about his sandwich.

"Perhaps I won't have my elevenses after all," he announced. "I don't want to spoil my picnic. Picnics make you hungry — especially when you have them out of doors!"